Christmas 2000

How wonderful to be together as a family. Once again at Olahis Haued—

Looking forward to the best Christmas ever.

Much love,
Mom (Oma) and
Dad (Papa)

GLORIA
THE CHRISTMAS ANGEL

A Story by Scott Anthony Asalone

Illustrated by Fibre Artist Mary Jo Scandin

DEDICATIONS

To my Grandfather, Patrick O'Connor,
who taught me the magic of storytelling.
SAA

To angels everywhere, young and old, large and small,
many of whom I've known.
MJS

T R E E H A U S
Treehaus Communications, Inc. P.O. Box 249 Loveland, OH 45140

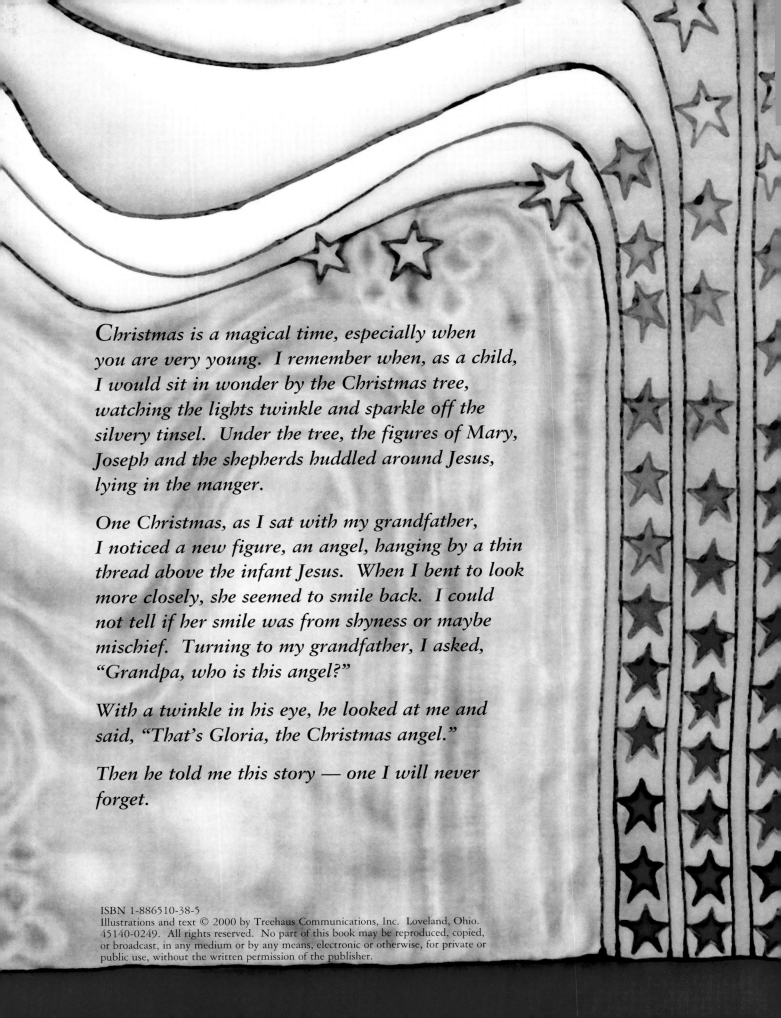

Christmas is a magical time, especially when
you are very young. I remember when, as a child,
I would sit in wonder by the Christmas tree,
watching the lights twinkle and sparkle off the
silvery tinsel. Under the tree, the figures of Mary,
Joseph and the shepherds huddled around Jesus,
lying in the manger.

One Christmas, as I sat with my grandfather,
I noticed a new figure, an angel, hanging by a thin
thread above the infant Jesus. When I bent to look
more closely, she seemed to smile back. I could
not tell if her smile was from shyness or maybe
mischief. Turning to my grandfather, I asked,
"Grandpa, who is this angel?"

With a twinkle in his eye, he looked at me and
said, "That's Gloria, the Christmas angel."

Then he told me this story — one I will never
forget.

ISBN 1-886510-38-5
Illustrations and text © 2000 by Treehaus Communications, Inc. Loveland, Ohio.
45140-0249.

It began a long time ago in heaven. The angels were practicing their songs. They knew that sometime soon God's Son was going to be born on earth. Gabriel, the Archangel, was pacing behind the choir. He was waiting for one absent angel. She was always late.

Suddenly, a spunky little angel flew round the corner. She crashed into Gabriel, sending them both tumbling into the clouds. Gabriel pushed her off himself and stood up. "Gloria," he said, frowning slightly, "you have to be more careful." He could not hide his frustration with Gloria. Her hair was a mess. Her halo was mended with masking tape. Her wings were bent so that she would fly first this direction, then that.

As Gabriel stared at her, Gloria could only think of how heavy her harp was to hold. Finally it slipped down — BANG! — right on Gabriel's foot. He cried out so loud in pain, it sounded like thunder.

"That's it," he said. "Go down to earth and don't come back until I call you."

With tears in her eyes, Gloria fluttered this way and that down to earth.

Meanwhile, in heaven, God was looking for an angel to do a special task.
(You see, when we're born, each of us has an angel to announce our birth.)
But God wanted a very special angel to announce the birth of God's Son.
So God wisely decided, "I will not let them know who this child is. I'll
only tell them that the child is from a very poor family. This way I will
find an angel who is just right."

God searched everywhere in
heaven for an angel to announce
the birth of a child who was poor.
But the angels all wanted to
announce the birth of God's Son.
They thought that if they accepted
to announce the birth of a poor
child, they might miss the chance
to tell of the Divine birth.

So they all pretended to be busy.
Each had an excuse not to go.
Some were shining stars.
Others were practicing hymns.
Still others were making clouds
and sending them into the sky.

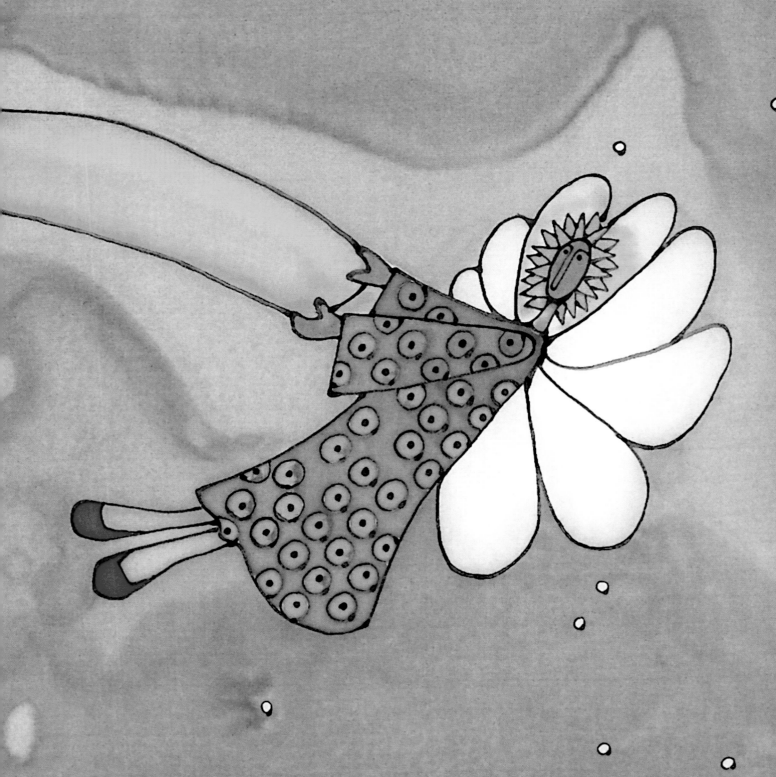

After walking all around heaven, God found no one who
wanted to announce a poor child's birth. "I will not pursue
it any further," God decided. "I am sure a worthy angel
will be found to announce the birth of my Son."

Meanwhile, on earth, Gloria was
still upset about being thrown
out of heaven. Her eyes were so
filled with tears, she could barely
see where she was flying, and she
crashed into the wall of a barn.
"Ouch!" she said, rubbing her
halo. "This is dangerous. I
should watch where I'm going."

She straightened herself and was
about to fly away when she heard
the cry of a baby. It came from
the barn. She flew in a window
to investigate.

Inside she found a young mother cuddling a new born baby in her arms. Gloria's eyes glowed at the beautiful sight. Then she noticed. "Why isn't an angel here to announce the birth of this child?" she said to herself.

She flew over to look more closely when, suddenly, her eyes and wings opened wide and she gasped in surprise.

"This is God's Son!" she exclaimed in a whisper.

At first Gloria didn't know what to do. Filled with joy, she flew this way and that inside the barn. With her crooked wings, she kept crashing into things. Trying to calm herself, she said, "I must tell someone about this!"

With a quick turn, she flew out of the barn to tell anyone she could find.

Nearby, she saw shepherds on a hillside tending their sheep. Short on breath, she tried to tell them. But Gloria was so small, the shepherds thought she was a bothersome bug and swished her away.

"I need something to get their attention," Gloria said to herself.

Gathering all her angel strength, Gloria flew high into the sky. She grabbed two stars, carried them above the shepherds, and — KABOOM! — crashed them together. The night sky exploded with light, filling all heaven and earth.

The shepherds trembled in fear as
Gloria's huge shadow spread across
the hills.   She drew in a deep breath
and called out: "Fear not, for behold
I bring you tidings of great joy!"

Then she told them the good news of God's love.

Meanwhile, from high in heaven, the angels rushed down to see what all the earthly excitement was about. There they discovered Gloria announcing the birth of God's Son.

"Glory to God in heaven!" they sang. "And peace on earth to all who are pleasing to God!"

And God was so pleased with Gloria that God decided she should never be forgotten.

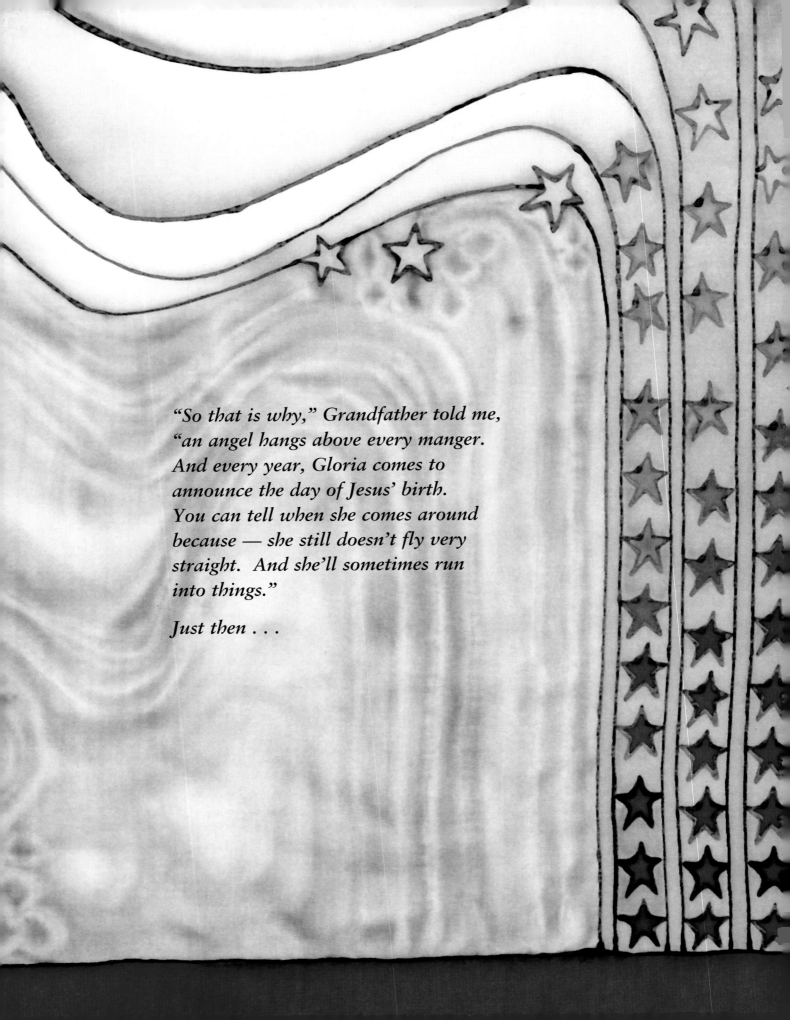

"So that is why," Grandfather told me, "an angel hangs above every manger. And every year, Gloria comes to announce the day of Jesus' birth. You can tell when she comes around because — she still doesn't fly very straight. And she'll sometimes run into things."

Just then . . .

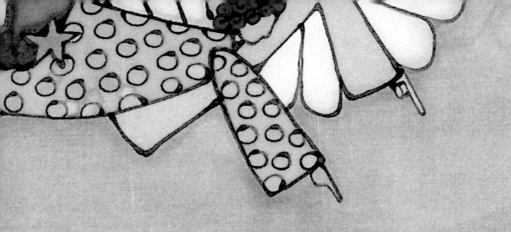

. . . a shiny ornament shook and fell from the tree.